It's a Fair Day, Amber Brown

PAULA DANZIGER

Illustrated by **Tony Ross**

G. P. Putnam's Sons · New York

G. P. Putnam's Sons, Reg. U.S. Pat. & Tm. Off. Published simultaneously in Canada.
Printed in Hong Kong by South China Printing Co. (1988) Ltd.
Designed by Gunta Alexander. Text set in Calisto.

Library of Congress Cataloging-in-Publication Data
Danziger, Paula, 1944– It's a fair day, Amber Brown / Paula Danziger;
illustrated by Tony Ross. p. cm. — (A is for Amber) Summary: Upset with her
parents for arguing on what she hoped would be a perfect day, Amber gets lost at
a county fair when she tries to follow her best friend Justin and his family through
the crowd. [1. Lost children—Fiction. 2. Fairs—Fiction. 3. Parent and child—Fiction.
4. Best friends—Fiction. 5. Friendship—Fiction. 6. Only child—Fiction.]
I. Ross, Tony, ill. II. Title. PZ7.D2394 Ir 2002   [Fic]—dc21 00-045973
ISBN 0-399-23606-6
1 3 5 7 9 10 8 6 4 2
First Impression

To Donna Larson –P. D.

I, Amber Brown, wake up

and hope that today is going to be a perfect day.

Yesterday was not a perfect day.

My mom and dad were angry at each other.

I, Amber Brown, hate when that happens.

I get dressed.

I put on all my good-luck things

to start a perfect vacation day.

As I walk downstairs,

I make sure that the back of my right shoe

touches each step.

When it touches each step, I say,

"Perfect day, perfect day."

Everyone is already in the kitchen,

talking and laughing—

Mom, Dad, my best friend, Justin Daniels,

his parents and his little brother, Danny.

We are all staying together in the Poconos.

Justin and I call it the Poke-a-Nose.

It looks like the beginning of a perfect day.

I pick up the box of Crunchie Munchies,
my favorite cereal.

It feels empty. I shake it. No sound.

I look inside. It's empty. I look inside again.

"Someone's eaten all of my cereal."

"Goldilocks and the three bears," Danny yells.

Everyone laughs except me.

What if not having my favorite cereal

means that today is not going to be a perfect day?

I, Amber Brown, look at the table.

Justin's bowl is overflowing with Crunchie Munchies.

Justin burps.

"Justin," his mother says.

I cross my eyes at him and oink.

He makes a funny face.

I oink again.

He makes another funny face.

I bet that he thinks I am going to just forget

that he's eaten all of my cereal . . .

and maybe ruined a perfect day.

Well, he's not only a pig. He's a pig in trouble.

"I wanted to eat some and then make a necklace
out of some of them," I say.

"Girls." Justin puts a spoonful of
Crunchie Munchies in his mouth.
He reaches over and takes food off Danny's plate.
"Why don't you just make a necklace
out of toaster waffles?"

Sometimes he just drives me nuts.

At home in New Jersey,

Justin and I are best friends.

We live next door to each other.

I am an only child.

Here in the Poconos,

we are all in the same house

and I don't feel like an only child.

Justin slurps the milk in his bowl.

I make myself a peanut butter

and jelly sandwich . . .

and ignore Justin.

Danny twirls around the room,

pretending to be a top.

I ignore him too.

My dad stands up.

"I'll go to the store and pick up

more Crunchie Munchies for Amber."

"Philip. Sit down," my mother says.

"I know what you are up to.

You want to go to the grocery store

so that you can call work.

This is your vacation. Relax."

My dad sits down again and sighs.

I sit down and start eating my sandwich.

Justin looks at me and crosses his eyes.

I cross my eyes back at him.

Then I look at my parents.

My dad looks as if he is trying hard

to stay in his seat and not call the office.

My mom looks as if she's trying hard

not to be annoyed that my dad

wants to call the office on his vacation.

But I know she is.

I cross my fingers and make a wish

that my parents don't get into a fight.

Then I put my head down on the table.

I hear the sound of something

scraping across the table toward me.

I lift my head and look.

It is the rest of Justin's cereal.

"Let's share," he says.

"I'll eat a toaster waffle instead."

The bowl is filled with soggy cereal.

I, Amber Brown, like to put a little milk on top

and eat it fast while it is still crispy.

16

My mom passes the bowl back to Justin.

"That's very nice of you, Justin,

but it's not very healthy."

It's a good thing that my mom doesn't know

that sometimes at school,

Justin and I share a piece of bubble gum . . .

after it has already been in one of our mouths.

I smile at Justin slurping milk out of his bowl.

He smiles back.

Justin's dad says, "Let's hurry up.

We should leave soon for the fair."

The county fair . . . rides and games and lots of food.

I, Amber Brown, am so excited.

"Look, Danny," I say, "that sign says

'Welcome to the County Fair.'"

"I can count." Danny jumps up and down.

"One, two, seven, four, eleven."

"County." I try to explain. "Not counting."

"County! County!" Danny jumps up and down again.

"One-y, two-y, seven-y, four-y, eleven-y."

Justin looks at his little brother.

"Garbanzo-bean brain."

"Justin," Mr. Daniels says. "No name-calling."

We go into the fair.

"Cotton candy!" Danny runs over to the booth.

We all follow.

"I'll buy one for each of us," my dad says.

"That stuff is disgusting," my mom says.

My dad buys it anyway.

My mom throws hers in the garbage.

Suddenly, my cotton candy doesn't taste so good.

We go to the barns.

The animals are cute, but the barn stinks . . .

sort of like Danny when he needs

to have his diaper changed.

Like now.

"Look at the load that tractor is hauling,"
my dad says, pointing to a huge machine.
"Kind of like my brother," Justin says,
holding his nose.
Mrs. Daniels picks up Danny
and takes him off to change him.

Justin and his dad go to ride the roller coaster.

I, Amber Brown, do not like the roller coaster.

My parents and I walk toward the merry-go-round.

My parents aren't talking.

I, Amber Brown, talk a lot to make up for the quiet.

"You know, when you are my size,

you see a lot of kneecaps and rear ends."

"Amber." My mom laughs. "That's not very polite."

"But it's very true," I say.

My dad kneels down

until he's about my size and looks around.

"You're right, Amber. Sarah, take a look.

Knees and rears."

My mom looks down at both of us and joins us.

This is the best time we've all had together

since the vacation started.

They stand up and I am left alone

in a world of knees and rears.

We get to the merry-go-round.

I want us all to sit together in the sleigh.

"Let's leave that for the little kids," Mom says.

Mom and Dad get on separate animals.

I get on a lion and pretend to lie down on it.

"Look! I'm lying on a lion . . . and I'm not lying . . .

I'm telling the truth."

"And our animals are all on a line,"

Mom says, laughing.

The merry-go-round starts and I pretend
to be Amber, Queen of the Jungle.

The merry-go-round stops and we all get off.

Neither of my parents looks at the other.

Neither is saying anything.

Maybe that's better than fighting,

but it's definitely not perfect.

"We're back," Justin says, coming up

with the rest of the Daniels family.

"Hot dogs," Justin says, pointing to a booth.

We all get hot dogs.

I name mine Rover and then I can't eat it.

My dad eats Rover.

I'll never name a hot dog again.

Then Danny grabs Justin's hand and points.

"Airplane. We ride."

I want to ride with Justin,

but sometimes he has to do things with Danny.

They get into their plane first.

Then I get into the plane behind them

with a little girl who doesn't have a partner.

Justin turns and yells,

"Boys against the girls. It's a race!"

Sometimes he is very silly.

They're in front. They're going to win.

The ride starts.

The planes leave the ground.

Faster . . . faster . . . the planes tilt to the side.

Faster . . . faster . . . the planes tilt a little more.

The little girl keeps going, "Varoom . . . beep, beep."

The planes start to slow down.

As each one reaches the platform, kids get off.

Justin and Danny get off ahead of us.

I just know that he's going to say he won.

I take a close look.

Justin does not look happy, even though he "won."

In fact, he looks very unhappy.

He has throw-up all over him.

Danny has throw-up coming out of his mouth
and all over his clothes.

Mrs. Daniels takes one look at them and says,

"Let's go back to the car and get a change of clothes . . .
and no more food for either of you."

"We'll be back soon," Mr. Daniels yells

over to my parents. They wave and nod.

Mom and Dad look like they are having a big talk.

They are not smiling.

I walk over to my parents.

They don't see me.

I, Amber Brown, see and hear them.

They have angry voices.

I, Amber Brown, hate angry voices,

especially from my mom and dad.

If they are going to fight,

I am going back to the car with the Danielses.

I walk away.

They still don't see me.

I keep walking.

I see a lot of knees and rears.

I can't remember how to get to the car.

I don't see anything that I remember.

I am getting scared.

This is a very big fair.

I am getting more scared . . . and more upset.

I am very lost.

I want my mom and dad . . . and I want them now.

I start to cry.

Tears are coming down my face

and gunk is coming out of my nose.

I, Amber Brown, don't even have a tissue.

I see a family eating at a picnic table.

I go over and ask them where the cars are.

The mom asks me if I am lost.

I nod and cry more.

The dad says,

"Wait here. I'll go and get some help."

The mom takes out a tissue and wipes my eyes.

She gives me one and I wipe my nose.

The dad comes back with a policeman.

"We'll take you to the lost-and-found tent,"

the policeman says. "Don't worry.

We'll find your family."

I thank the family and wave good-bye.

The policeman takes me to a tent.

"Will the parents of Amber Brown please come

to the lost-and-found tent by the front entrance,"

a lady says over a loudspeaker.

In a few minutes, my mom and dad rush in.

They pick me up and hug me.

I'm crying. My mom is crying . . .

and I think my dad is trying not to cry.

"I was so scared," we all say at once.

Mom sniffles. "Amber, honey,

we thought you were with the Danielses.

When they came back without you,

we were so worried. We've been looking

everywhere for you."

"You were fighting," I said.

"So I went to look for them."

My mom and dad look at me

and then at each other

and then back at me.

They say how sorry they are

and hug me all over again.

The Danielses rush over.

We hug . . . except for Justin.

He just makes a face and I make a face back.

Then our families make plans to meet in an hour.

The Danielses go to the farm machines.

We go to the game booths.

I hold hands with my mom and dad

and think about being so happy

that it will spread to them.

"Look," Dad says. "Basketball.

I used to be very good at this."

We walk to the booth.

My father puts money down

and picks up a basketball.

One ball in.

Two balls in.

Three in and he wins.

I jump up and down.

For my prize I pick a big, fluffy pencil.

My dad plays again.

He wins again.

This time he picks the prize.

It's a teddy bear holding a heart.

Dad gives it to Mom.

They are smiling at each other,

and that makes me happy.

We play more games.

I, Amber Brown, throw coins and win two goldfish.

Mom, Dad and I all play the squirt game.

Some big boy wins.

A little girl cries because she loses.

I, Amber Brown, give her one of my goldfish.

I am an only child who will be happy

with an only goldfish.

The little girl is so happy.

So am I.

Today a Fair Day

turned into an almost-perfect day.